I0760512

Also by Mark Binder

Fictions for Adults

Loki Ragnarok
A Dead Clam, an Undead Politician, and an Ancient Horror
The Buddha Who Wore Keds
Crumbs Don't Count (The Rationalization Diet)

Groston Adventures

The Zombie Cat
It Ate My Sister
It was a dark and stormy night… (live audio)

Life in Chelm

The Brothers Schlemiel
A Hanukkah Present
Matzah Mishugas

Traditional and Original Tales

Transmit Joy! (audio)
Cinderella Spinderella
Every Hero Has a Story
The Bed Time Story Book
Tall Tales, Whoppers and Lies (live audio)
Classic Stories for Boys and Girls (audio)
Kings, Wolves, Princesses and Lions
Genies, Giants and a Walrus
A Holiday Present (live audio)

Loki Ragnarok

Mark Binder

Light Publications
Providence

Contents

Loki – The Trickster

Gods

Odin – Father of the Aesir, Blood Brother to Loki
Thor – The Thunder God
Freya – The Fair. Odin's wife
Frigg – Mother of Baldur
Idun – Keeper of the golden apples of youth
Baldur – Handsome and Beloved
Hod – Baldur's blind brother
Heimdall – The Watchman
Tyr – One-armed Swordsman
Sif – Thor's wife

Loki's Family

Fenris – The wolf. Loki's son.
Jormungand – The Midgard serpent. Loki's son.
Hel – Ruler of the underworld. Loki's daughter.
Angrboda – Loki's mistress. A giant. Mother of Fenris, Jormungand and Hel.
Sigyn – Loki's wife. Mother of Nari and Narfi
Slepnir – An eight-legged horse. Loki's son.

Giants and More

Snorri – a bricklayer
Svaldifari – Snorri's horse
Skadi – a giantess
Thiazi – a giant. A thief. Father of Skadi.
Vanir – rivals defeated by Odin
Vala – a seeress
Norns – three witches

Setting

Asgard – home of the gods
Yggdrasil – the world tree from which all the nine known worlds grow
Bifrost Bridge – path between worlds
Midgard – the land of men
Jotunheim – the land of giants
Niflheim – the underworld
Valhalla – Odin's hall in Asgard, where gods and dead heroes feast. A bit of a dump.

Loki's Saga

This tale I tell began long before time, and will not finish until the last coals of creation burn to smoldering dust.

This is a tale of gods and giants,
of ice and fire.

Of the world of men, small though they be,
unmatched in their scrabbling, scratching, fighting,
clawing, biting, hacking their way into the brief
and glorious light of the sun before their flimsy
candles are snuffed,
extinguished,
and darkness is all once more.

This is the tale of Ragnarok, the end of the world,
the end of time.
The great and glorious battle between the giants
and the gods –
Ragnarok.

It begins…

The Prophecy

Ages ago, when the world was young,
Odin went to the seeress, Vala,
and asked her,
"What will come?"

Odin, the allfather, lord of the Aesir,
seeker of truth.
Thor's sire, Baldur's father,
Loki's brother in blood.

Ages ago
or was it yesterday?
Odin, who gave up one of his eyes for knowledge,
Hung himself upside down by his foot
for nine days upon Yggdrasil,
The tree of the world,
hoping to learn all.

Odin
the damned fool
asked Vala, the seer,
to scry him the future.
What a fucking idiot.

For she told.
Vala told Odin.
Told of the beginnings,
of the creation of the nine worlds,
the birth of the gods and the giants and men.

Vala foretold the great days
when the gods ruled the nine worlds.
But Vala did not stop there.
She told him.
He told us in Asgard.
Told us of the doom
Told of the death
Told the destruction, devastation, desecration,
demolition
The demise of all we know.
All we love.

Once you set a prophecy in motion,
like a sled racing down a the side of a cliff,
you cannot hop off in the middle
but must ride it through,
beyond frolic and fun,
past pleasure,
into fear,
through terror,
until the end.

So, Odin asked and Vala told, and
from the beginning, from the first days,
we knew our time was limited.
Set, like an hourglass
sifting away the moments invisibly,
until at last, the last,
gone!

Vala told Odin
and Odin told all
of Ragnarok.
Ragnarok, the battle at the end of time,
when gods battle giants,
and win not.

We will know it is neigh,
when brave Baldur dies.
When three winters, dark and cold,
arrive without summers in between.
When the wolf Fenris breaks his bonds,
and swallows the sun.
When the earth shudders.
When the seas foam and then freeze.
When Heimdall sounds his echoing horn thrice
Ragnarok begins.

So, from the beginning we knew it all.
Baldur's demise.
Odin's wolf-torn doom.
The bitch Vala even told how many steps
Thor, hammerslinger, would take before
collapsing, melting to the earth, drenched
in the poison of the world serpent's blood.
Nine. Nine steps.

And, from the beginning of days I knew.
          Vala said.
My son, Fenris, a good dog but woefully
misunderstood,
will slay Odin,
          Vala said.
Another son, Jormungand, the serpent who
encircles the world,
never much for brains but a heart the size of an
island,
Jormungand will rise from the deep,
and gnaw his way through Thor's thunder thighs.
The seeress told that.
          Vala said.
Loki himself is to be bound to a rock,
tied by his firstborn son's intestines,
while a snake's acid venom drips searing drops
into Loki's once lovely visage.

Vala said.
Loki's noble wife, Sigyn, holds a cup to catch the
poison. But the cup fills and Sigyn must empty it
every so often. And then, as the vile burning poison
falls from the snake's fangs, Loki screams to the
heavens, shaking the earth with his quakes of pain.

How'd you like to wake up every morning
wondering when that shit was going to start?

That's the trouble with prophecy.
It's all so fucking certain.

All it takes is one feeble withered crone to foretell
the gods that their world is due for destruction
and that my children will cause it.
Ruined my life, my family, that soothsayer did.

You know what else she said of me?
In the end, on the eve of Ragnarok
I would be freed. Freed at last.
That I would ride out of Niflheim, my daughter,
Hel's domain, on a ship made from the fingernails
of the dead.

I like that, don't you?

Mad Loki
a lunatic, howling like his son the dog, gibbering,
baying,
completely insane,
sailing across heaving frozen waters
on a great barge of glued-together
fungus-encrusted fingernails.
It appeals to my sense of humor.

And the next thing you know,
it's time.
Time!
The signs are upon us.
Three frozen winters have we now seen
without a summer in between.

I am rockbound no more.
The scars burned into my cheeks still sear,
but I stand.
Listen. In the distance hear you the baying?
My son, the wolf Fenris, the dog of war,
straining at his leash,
howls through his pierced jaws
as he waits for dawn
when he will eat the sun.
The triple winter is upon us.

Hear you Heimdall's horn?
The armies are assembling.
Soon the carnage will begin.
And I
and all that I love
will be slain.

All it takes is one feeble withered crone to foretell
the gods that their world is due for destruction,
and that my children will cause it.
Ruined my life, my family, that soothsayer did.

And all thanks to Odin's foreknowing thirst.

Now I have one simple question.
Tell me true, wise all-knowing old bastard.
What of Loki, your blood brother,
What of Loki's children?
Odin, tell Loki, your playmate from birth, how to
avoid this prophecy!

No?
Your ancient mouth remains shut?
So it is said, so it will pass.

That's the problem knowing the future,
it's all so damned certain.

Ahh, well.
The night is long my children.
The fire still burns.
In the space of a few short hours we will drink
and laugh,
feast and plot,
love, fight, die and live.
For now.

On the eve of battle
is the time to tell tales,
sing ballads, glorious stories,
remembering, reliving, reveling
in all that has been.

Tomorrow all ends in blood.
All dead. All cold.
Still, we have tonight yet to be told.

By the Ruins of Asgard

When the world was younger,
long before Ragnarok,
we had just fought a war with the Vanir.
We won, of course,
but at such a terrible cost.

Asgard was in ruins.
The city of the gods lay in rubble, its great walls demolished.
The compromise with the Vanir,
their joining together with the Aesir,
did us no good.
Gods, like men, are lazy sorts, given to galloping around,
drinking and boasting, fighting and destruction,
but not much in the way of the practical.

So, inside the great hall of Valhalla,
the gods gathered to discuss the wasteland outside,
and lay plans for its renewal.
They formed planning committees,
subcommittees, investigative committees,
design, decoration, planting and building committees.

Everyone was on a committee,
and of course nothing got done.
Daily we made our way to the hall,
clambering across the great cracked boulders,
the crushed walls, the crumbled gates of Asgard.
And we talked. And talked. And drank.
And talked and talked and talked and talked and
talked and talked and talked. And drank.

Until one day, a man came riding across the
Bifrost Bridge.

Small fellow with rotten teeth and a scrawny horse,
a pale scraggly beard on both the horse and the man.
Heimdall, the wakeful watchman, stopped him cold
And asked after the weather in Midgard.

Not one for small talk, the man got straight to the point. "I am Snorri, the master builder. I demand to see the gods."

Heimdall laughed, but Snorri said he would not budge until he had an audience with the gods.

For nine days Snorri stood fast by the bridge,
sweating in the sun,
his bony horse foraging among the rocks.

At last, Loki, the crafty and cunning, asked,
"Why is that festering man-shaped dung heap standing by the side of the Bifrost Bridge? Can't someone clean it up?"

Steadfast Heimdall squinted at Loki,
and explained the man's strange request.

"Are we," asked Loki, "to permit this derelict to rot on the edge of our realm? Bring him in so we can kick his scrawny ass back to Midgard!"

Another committee was formed, and after much debate, the man was escorted into the presence of the wise and powerful gods.

Such was the man's stench that Loki held his nose.
Thor coughed into his red beard.
Odin the Allfather stopped his own breath.
And fair Freya, most beautiful of the goddesses,
veiled her lovely face to mask the fumes.

"Snorri," said Loki. "Tell us why you should live."

Odin frowned at Loki's presumption to speak for the gods, but as he had no breath, Odin spoke not a word.

"I will rebuild the walls around Asgard," said the unwashed man.

As he spoke, the wind from his lips blew the stink of the ages among the gods.
So foul was this corruption,
that beside it, rotten eggs, raw sewage
and vomitus bile would smell sweet.

Baldur, fairest and most beloved of the gods,
turned a grim shade of green
and stumbled from the assembly hall,
his exit soon punctuated by the piteous sounds of retching.

"Outline your plan," grinned Loki.
"What do you propose? Tell us your price."
"But be brief," thundered Thor, "if you value your life."

"I will build the wall in eighteen months," said Snorri. Even these few words caused a cascade of convulsions among the Aesir. "All I ask is for the sun and the moon and the hand of fair Freya."

At this last request, Freya, the object of Snorri's base lust, rose from her unsteady seat.

Though her intestines were churning with nauseous revulsion, Freya looked fabulous as she swept from the room with dignity and grace, and left the meeting hall.
Her silent exit, a clear "no" to the builder's thick desire.

Snorri sighed as the object of his affection passed from his sight, and that whiff of Snorri's excrable breath was more than the gods could bear.

With one swift motion, Thor grabbed the man's scrawny neck and booted him firmly out the door.

Snorri flew high through the sky,
and would have splattered on the rocks,
had he not landed by chance,
on the bony back of his broken down nag.

Though the builder was gone, his scent lingered.
Coughs and sputters filled the hall.
Odin burned a sprig of mistletoe
as incense to clear the air.

When at last the stench had been banished,
Loki looked at his queasy kindred and said,
"I like him. I think we should give it a try."

The roars of the gods were deafening.
Loki laughed, sneering at their lazy innocence.
"What's the harm? One man rebuild the walls of
Asgard in eighteen months time? Absurd.
It would take nine gods with the strength of Thor
twice that length just to clear the rubble."

"Then why," asked Odin, breathing easily now that
the stench had cleared, "even consider the matter?"

"At least it's a start," answered foxy Loki.
"Maybe he'll build us a tower, an outhouse.
A bathhouse with water that runs and a tub we
can throw him into."

Another committee was formed. Arguments
heard. Freya refused to consider the contract.
Loki, the master negotiator, held firm.
He begged, pleaded, rebutted, and cajoled.
At last Loki devised terms, and Freya agreed.

Noses hidden behind sweet-scented handkerchiefs,
the gods traveled forth from their great hall, and met
with the beggar builder beside the Bifrost Bridge.

"We have considered your offer," spoke Odin,
"and agree…"

“But under these conditions,” interrupted Loki, who then stopped cold, withering under the Allfather’s glare.

Odin continued, “The sun, the moon, and the hand of fair Freya will be yours, but only if you finish the wall in nine month’s time.”

The reeking rebuilder opened his mouth to protest, but Thor quickly clamped a thick hand firmly over Snorri’s foul maw.

“You must work alone,” Odin said, voicing Loki’s proviso. “At the end of nine months, if the wall is unfinished, your life is forfeit.”

“But either way you have to take a bath,” added Loki.

“Wait,” Thor said, holding his huge palm firm across Snorri’s cesspool lips. “Say not a word. Open not your mouth. Simply shake your head, no or yes.”

Snorri looked as thoughtful as any man could with the god of thunder smothering him.
His life wagered against the sun and the moon and such beauty?

Snorri nodded his head, and Thor removed his hand, wiping his fingers in the dirt to cleanse them of Snorri's spittle.

"But I will need my horse, Svaldifari," Snorri said.

Despite their handkerchiefs, the gods sputtered and gasped.
"No!" bellowed Odin.

"Let him use the nag," coughed Loki. "Anything to close his mouth and get him off our doorstep."

Without pause for debate, a vote was taken.
All voted "Aye."
All save Baldur, the brave but weak-stomached, again too busily wracked, retching his breakfast behind a rosebush.

"We agree," said Odin. "Is the deal struck?"

Lightning fast, Thor raised his hand and then closed it into a fist. "Nod aye or shake nay, lest I slay thee this instant."

Snorri gazed at lovely Freya and, without hesitation, nodded his assent.

Then, with joyful glee, Loki dumped a barrel of ice water over the heads of the skinny man and his starving steed and shouted, "Get to it!"

Woeful and wet, Snorri and his horse stumbled off to gather their tools.

The next morning, hours before dawn,
a roar louder than thunder awakened the gods.
Thinking that Thor's great chariot had lost a wheel
the gods rushed to their windows.

There in the light of the fading moon
they saw Snorri and his horse Svaldifari
dragging across the plains of Ida
a great net filled with boulders that rumbled
as they rolled into a pile the size of a small
mountain.

As the golden tresses of sunlight at last glimmered
on the horizon, the gods saw the small builder
tossing the boulders as if they were pebbles,
and slapping them firmly into place with mortar.

Work on the walls had begun.
And in their hearts, the gods felt the first
stabbings of doubt.

Days passed.
Each morning the gods' restful sleep was destroyed by the crashing avalanche pulled by the bony broken dray horse Svaldifari.

Though small and weak in appearance, and dwarfed beside the very slabs of stone it towed, not once did the nag stumble or stall.

"We have been cheated," said Baldur, the best beloved of all the gods, careful to stay upwind from the builder.

Frigg, Baldur's mother, agreed.
"That horse is enchanted," she said.
"And that pathetic man, Snorri, is as strong as Thor."
The thunder god snorted his disgust.

"Perhaps," said Loki, squinting at the workman, "Snorri is a giant in disguise."

"A giant!" boomed Thor. "You pledged our lovely Freya to a giant?"

"Relax," replied Loki, stepping back out of Thor's reach. "The task is barely begun. Nine months is too short even for a giant and a determined dragon."

"First a giant, now a dragon?" Thor bellowed.
But Loki ducked away, and was gone
before Thor's temper could pound him into eternity.

Days became weeks, weeks became months,
and the end of the nine-month term drew close.

Each dawn, the gods,
cranky and exhausted from broken sleep,
gathered to watch Snorri and Svaldifari's progress.
The laughter and mirth had drained from their faces.
The halls of Valhalla were silent and glum.

Loki, of course, was nowhere to be found.
He was taking his ease in his mistress's hut.

"We shall lose all to that deceitful giant," moaned Baldur. "What good are walls without the light of the sun, and the bright of the moon, and the warm glow from fair Freya's face?"

"Why so grim?" said a voice at last.

All turned to see Loki sitting on one of the new walls, rested and refreshed, his legs dangling and kicking like a lively young boy.

Odin, Loki's brother in blood,
snatched his sibling down from his perch.

"Ow!" yelled the crafty one. "Calm yourselves.
I have a plan."

"You had best," whispered Odin, his thumb and forefinger digging painfully into the lobe of Loki's ear, until the shape shifter changed his form into a puddle of water and dribbled onto the ground.

Loki reconstituted himself,
held his hands aloft and said,
"The bet is as good as won.
Snorri's wall will not be completed.
The sun and the moon will chase each other
through the sky.
And fair Freya will evermore bless us with her
beauty."

"If not," Odin said, "we will take you apart piece
by piece."

Then Thor, as if to demonstrate,
lifted a rock the size of a house,
and slowly tore off hunks
before powdering them between his fingers.

Loki winced once, then winked, and was away.

Next morning, when Snorri led Svaldifari to the site,
another horse, a handsome brown mare, pranced
beside the nearly-completed stone walls.
She was as beautiful a horse as the nine worlds had
ever seen, with a long smooth mane, a powerful
back, strong neck, and good teeth.

Svaldifari, dedicated as he was to his master task,
was powerless to resist this gorgeous creature's
charms.

The mare pranced about, swishing her tail
and whinnying with a sweet nickering voice.
Svaldifari strained at his traces, shook his bit,
and whinnied back.

Though Snorri tried to control his steed, the
desires of nature were not to be denied.

Svaldifari neighed thrice, broke his tethers, yanked
the reins, and danced free beside the brown mare.

The two nuzzled for a moment,
before galloping off
to a distant and private wood.

Snorri, the builder, the long and hardworking mason,
stared at the broken leathers, looked to the last
incomplete gate, the only still-broken stretch of
the immense new walls that now surrounded
Asgard, and knew he'd been tricked.
Without his steed's help, finishing the job was
hopeless.

On top of the walls, were the gods,
looking down at Snorri with grins of relief.
Their laughter soon filled the air.

On that last evening of the final day of the ninth
month, Snorri stood before his unfinished walls
and tore off his disguise.

There stood revealed a stone giant,
as ugly and immense as his breath's stench.
"I had loved you Freya!" Snorri shouted.

But the goddess turned her head from the
foul-speaking wind.

And with one thundering blow,
Thor shattered the stone giant's skull.
The rock-like pieces of Snorri's body were used as
cobbles to line the road.

Secure now inside their nearly finished walls,
the gods raised their mugs in gleeful celebration.

All save Loki, who was not seen for many months.

When at last a year and a day had passed,
Loki the trickster returned.
Limping and pale,
he led behind him, along the newly cobbled road,
a young horse with eight legs.

"An interesting companion," said Odin, raising an eyebrow. "Is he yours?"

Loki winced at the insult.
"Yes, he is mine and Svaldifari's. I call him Slepnir."

"That makes Loki," sniggered Baldur, "a horses' ass."
Neither wit nor kindness were beautiful Baldur's lot.

But, as they often did, Baldur and the rest of the gods lifted their voices in laughter at Loki,
always at Loki.

"He looks like a fine steed," Odin grinned.

"I bore him for your sake," Loki said. "If he can
bear you, you can ride him.
He can run through the air and on top of water.
He will carry you all the way to the land of the dead.
And back. Perhaps."

The gods roared with laughter,
even Loki, sitting gingerly in his chair,
cracked a pained smile.

Thor handed the fox a mug of ale
And thanked the trickster for his tale.

Betrayals

Yes, I was cheating on my wife, Sigyn.
Sigyn was beautiful and gentle,
kind and comforting,
generous and a pretty good cook.
Gods, she was boring.

I like my women lusty, fiery, and fierce.
That was not my wife, alas.
So, awandering I went,
like every good god, in search of maidens fair and bawdy to share my bed and warm my heart.
Didn't find any.
Not in Asgard, the land of the gods,
though I sampled many – if not all – of heaven's secrets.
Not in Midgard, the world of men.
Oh, plenty of beauties I dallied with there,
but none long enough to catch my fancy for more than an hour, or quarter hour.
Not to pass judgment on all of humanity,
but your lives are so short and fragile
that you never seem worth much more than a spurt of the moment.

My lacivious journey took me at last to
my homeland, Jotunheim, land of the giants.

You must by now know that, though I keep
company with the gods, I am giantborne.
Is Loki a god? Giant? Neither one nor the other.
Though I live in the palace, I never forget the
farm, and from time to time I like to visit.
For one thing, returning to the old homeland
reminded me how kempt the gods keep Asgard.
Now that the walls were mostly fixed, there was
no litter. As the chair of the sanitation committee,
I made sure that the garbage was kept out back in
a heap, near Baldur's palace.

One day in Jotunheim I saw the wench Angrboda,
and I knew I had to have her.
She saw me coming, knew my position of power,
and played me like a giant sea bass.

"No, good sir Loki," she said, "I cannot tarry with
a married man."
"Man?" quoth I. "I'm more than a man, more
than a giant, more than a god."
"Are you as big as all that?"
"Bigger," I answered. "I am a shape changer.
Think about it."

She answered not, but blushed as red as a spring rose.
The haystack was not far afield and
soon we were tumbling and jumbling and
fumbling like children at play.
It felt good not to be nice or careful or gentle.
And she gave as good as she got.
WRrrah!

Fecund woman.
Caught my seed the first time around.
How many aeons had I slept with wifely Sigyn
and only produced those two bland nothings,
we called Nari and Narfi?
One quick tumble, and this giant wench's belly
swelled like a monstrous tumor.
It's always the way, isn't it?
Loki plays at horse just once as a favor to the gods
and carried Slepnir twelve months to pay the price.
Still, I couldn't stay away.
Even with the bitch breeding a brood,
Angrboda's charms had captured my heart,
or at least my lust.

Our firstborn was the wolf Fenris.
God, he was a good looking pup.
Eyes as red as coals,
teeth as sharp as a scorned wife's tongue,

jaws as strong as the stench from an unclean stable.
His howls to suck at his mam's tit could be heard
as far as Asgard.
We tussled, as Daddy and child are wont to do,
wrestled, hunted, played ball, fetch the stick.
I could toss an oak tree fifty miles,
he'd snap it before it hit the ground, and be back
at my side in a twinkle, panting for more.
Fenris was a good boy.
Good boy.

Our next born was Jormungand,
the snake, the serpent.
A bigger reptile the nine worlds have never seen.
When carrying this worm,
Angrboda nearly exploded.
Did she complain?
Is newly fallen snow white? Is pissed snow yellow?
Oh, my, yes.
"My back hurts, my belly is huge. I'm ugly."
And she was.
Her stomach was five hundred times bigger than
the rest of her.
Five hundred!
It was revolting.

Naturally I stayed far away.

You may think me a boor or a cad,
but when you look at a thing of beauty
distorted to such monstrous proportions,
it's a wonder I didn't slay her in her sleep.
Halfway around the world wasn't far enough
to avoid hearing her birthing cries.
She howled and moaned,
set the boy Fenris off, too,
and between the two of them,
that dire chorus kept the universe awake
for fifteen days and fifteen nights.

Disgusting process birth is, especially if you're
dropping a snake long enough to stretch from
horizon to horizon.

Not much you can do with a child like
Jormungand either.
You can't bounce him on your lap or play peek-a-boo.
He just lays there, all writhing and slithers.
Stupid as a plank.
One day I set out to look Jormy in the eye and
take his measure.
Took me two weeks to find the end and it turned
out to be the wrong one.

Even with Angrboda minding our bizarre menagerie,

I couldn't stay away from her.
No matter how I vowed,
my thoughts kept turning to her bountiful body,
her ample mountains, and her well-plowed field.

Truthfully, Sigyn had kicked me out of her bed
and I had nowhere else to sleep.

You would have thought that after
Jormungand and Fenris
enough was enough.
No, we were a fertile pair, Angrboda and I.

Our daughter, Hel,
slipped out as easily as quicksilver through
fingertips.

Hel was a tiny one, thin and wan,
skin white as bone,
eyes as pale as a moon-clouded sky.
And small.
A month after she was born,
she was still no larger than the palm of my hand.
Hel, my poor fragile baby daughter, was sickly
from birth.
Her fair skin. It was so lovely, at first.
Until it began to rot.

It flaked off in great black and grey festering clumps.
I can't tell you how I felt.
I would stare into her infant face,
so innocent and trusting,
knowing that despite all my powers
I could do nothing to ease her suffering and pain.

My daughter lived, but at what cost?
Hel grew, wise and tall,
but her body was a mass of green festering sores.

In the dark of night we, papa and daughter, could
talk for hours, but at the first light of dawn, when
my gaze fell on Hel's broken and scarred face,
father or not, I stepped outside to retch.

Desperate I was.
I went to the gods, and asked for a cure.
Perhaps Idun's golden apples of heaven would
restore Hel's health.
Certainly, Odin, the wise all-knowing master of
the nine worlds, must know some remedy.
I all but begged that he help his blood brother and
family.

One-eyed Odin said, "Aye"
But he lied.

Rather than assist Loki's daughter,
Odin went to the Norns to ask their advice.

Now, the Norns – Urd, Skuld and Verthandi –
Fate, Being and Necessity,
are three wicked witchy gossipy bitches,
as useless and dangerous as that cursed seer, Vala.
The Norns are withered crones dressed in rags,
eating raw bark from the roots of the world tree.
I could go on, but what's the point?

Did the Norns help Hel? Nay. Instead,
the hags reminded Odin of Vala's prophecy.

Urd called Angrboda a monster.
Skuld declared Loki was evil.
And Verthandi claimed that Loki's kinder clung to
the worst of both parents.

When the world ends, the Norns retold,
Loki's offspring would stand on the side of
destruction and slay the gods.
Fenris would devour Odin,
Jormungand would slay Thor.
Hel would ride from the Underworld on the
fingernails of the dead…

Blah blah blah blah blah blah blah.
Prophecy? Nonsense!
Complete rubbish.
If you'd seen those kids, my children,
beautiful babies all,
(except Jorgy, and what can you expect from a
giant snake?)
you would have known that there was no evil
born in them. None born.
None, but what was put in there by prophesy.

The fact that no one, myself included,
had remembered one word of this prophetic
nonsense, until the Norns again raised the issue,
ought to have been proof enough
that it was all lies.

Odin and his gods, however, believed the bull,
bought the bitches' blather, and blamed my bairn.

They call themselves gods.
Rulers of the heavens, and nine worlds.
Scared kittens. Cowering mice.
Terrified insects.
Frightened of three little children.

It had all been forgotten!

But I, Loki the wily, Loki the cunning,
Loki the fool,
had reminded it to them.

That very night, under the cover of darkness,
while my children and their mother slept,
Odin slunk forth from Asgard
and sneaked into Jotunheim.
He crept to the house that Angrboda kept,
and lurked outside, waiting until the silent hour
of death.
Then, in an instant,
Odin burst in, through the doors,
binding first the mother of my children,
gagging her mouth, so she could watch with
horror but utter not a sound.
He stole our children before Angrboda's eyes,
while she writhed in the dirt with rage insane.

Jormungand, Odin tossed into the oceans,
hurling my idiot snake of a son into the icy seas
to sink to the bottom and drown.
Jormungand did not die. His fate was crueler.
He lived under the sea, and grew.
And grew and grew and grew. And grew.
His eyes never again would witness bright
summer's light, but his body grew longer and

longer, until at last he encircled the world.
When his mouth met his other tip, howling
outrage Jormungand tried to swallow himself.
Ended up gagging on his own tail.
Poor stupid beast.

My waif, my innocent,
my tortured tiny Hel,
Odin too tossed away.
To Niflheim, the world of the dead, he sent her.
A living breathing child Odin banished from
the face of the earth, to live among the cold and
decayed.
Heroes die and are reborn in Valhalla. The rest rot.
Hel's playmates were the worm and maggot-eaten
corpses of the sickly and feeble,
of any who perished from illness or old age.

My baby grew up quickly in Niflheim, and fancied
herself a princess born to rule the underworld.
A chorus of carcass courtiers built her a castle of
mud and grave dirt.
They fed her from the plate of hunger with the
knife of famine.
My poor child. My poor little girl.
Ahh, I suppose she made the best of the
circumstances.

So I kicked it.
A great mistake.

Only momentary was the pause.
Then away went the goat, and I no choice but to
follow, shouting a song that sounded like,
"YEEEeeeEEEeeeEEE! YAAWK
ReeWWOOOOooWOOO!"

The cask I dared not drop, for its ale was priceless.
The umbrella I could not drop, for without its drag,
that goat might have launched me over a cliff.

Here the goat ran. There the goat darted.
And close behind, yanked and jerked along,
followed I, stumbling and fumbling, feet flailing.
Eyes goggled. Face blue. Balls bluer.

That billy goat jumped at every dog.
It raced through every stream,
up every hill, along every narrow cliff trail.

At last, when it seemed I could give chase no more
The wretched baahbarian stopped cold and once
again began munching on shoots.
Slowly, carefully, quietly I crept up behind the goat.
Yes, I should have set down the ale and umbrella

and whipped out my knife, but in my distraught
state of mind I was committed, unable to let loose
my burdens.

Instead, I knelt down and gnawed gently
at the testicle-tied goat rope with my sharp teeth.

I was nearly through. Nearly done!
But, with only a single strand of string left,
the goat looked into my eye.
It knew.
I knew.
There was no time.

Instantly, I dropped the ale, let the umbrella go,
and snatched for the goat's collar.

The consequences were uprooting.

A gust of wind lifted the loosed umbrella like a
goosed ghost.
That spooked the goat, which darted off like a
rabbit chased by a hound.
The strand of rope once again pulled tighter than taut.
Unable to rise nor run, I was dragged along behind,
and screeched in distorted agony!
"YEEOOOWWWWWWWWWWWWWWKKKK!"

At last, the tether's final fiber snapped.
Loki collapsed.
The goat vanished into the hills.

Until dusk, I did lay in the dirt,
gathering my senses, exposed to the rain.
I drank the entire cask of ale.
Then, empty handed and wide-legged, I walked
all the way home on tiptoes to keep my balls from
dragging in the dirt.

"How did you feel?" Skadi asked.
"How?" I replied. "Tender testicles tormented
each step, along with an ale cask's urge to pause at
every tree. I was pissed!"

Did Skadi, the sad and mourning ice giantess,
laugh at Loki's crass misfortune?
Well, of course she did. She howled with glee until
crystal tears dripped from her eyes.

Honest laughter, that momentary loss of sense
and self, it is all that separates gods and giants and
men from the beasts of the earth.

All was well in Asgard now
As Loki took his well-deserved bow.

The Death of Baldur

Returned we triumphant from Skadi's laughing defeat. It should have been a joyous homecoming, filled with applause.

Once again, Loki had risked all (including his balls) to save and protect the Aesir from folly. Time at last for Loki to receive his due praise and thanks.

Yet in Asgard all was not as we had left.
The gods had conceived a new game.
They called it "Stoning Baldur."
The rules were simple. Each god took a turn hurling gigantic boulders at Baldur's head and Lo! he was unharmed.

Why was Odin's son, Baldur so protected?
Baldur the beautiful. Baldur the beloved.
Baldur the weak. Baldur the frightful.

Baldur had been having nightmares of doom and death, black lustful dreams filled with specters of Hel, my daughter, her underworld, and darkness.

When Odin, the Allfather, heard of this vision,
he traveled to Niflheim, the land of the dead,
and peered into the windows of Hel's dusky castle.

The floors had been covered with gold,
a silver cauldron bubbled at one end.
Mystified, Odin raised a spirit from the dead and
asked, "Why are the floors covered with gold?
What in that silver cauldron bubbles?"

"We await," said the spirit, "the arrival of Baldur.
The gold is to honor his presence. The cauldron
brews with ale to celebrate his end."

When Frigg, Baldur's mother, heard the news, she
screamed with fear.
Then Frigg set out to thwart her son's destiny.
To every plant, every creature, to every element in
all the nine worlds, Frigg traveled,
and begged that they forswear any harm to Baldur.

Cold iron swore never to hurt the pretty Baldur.
Lions gave their promises as well.
No claw, no fang would pierce Baldur.
Rock and eagle, ice and mouse, all agreed.
Large and small, every single chip of stone,
vegetable and being that breathed, all agreed,

Baldur would be safe.

So arose the game, a game that Loki would have
been proud to call his own, of hurling first sticks and
then spears, then logs at Baldur the Beautiful,
and watching them, like acorns off rooftops, bounce.

Thor was the last to put Baldur to the test.
His blow with the hammer Mjölnir
smashed Baldur full force in the skull.
The beautiful one smiled unblinking.
Then the Thunder God laughed and declared
"With Baldur the invulnerable on our side,
the giants will do naught but die
when Ragnarok arrives."

To one side stood Loki.
Triumphant Loki, ignored Loki, watching this
mindless fun.

They hit Baldur with shovels, with cooking pots,
sides of beef, and a half-smoked salmon.
Baldur roared in joy, as if tickled with a feather.

So, disguised as an old woman, Loki went to Frigg.
"Ohh, what a racket, we passed on the road," said
Loki. "Who could be making such ruckus, and why?"

Smug, Frigg told this helpless old woman of her quest, of the promises extracted from every creature, every thing, protecting her son Baldur from harm.

"Every creature?" said crone-visaged Loki. "Even the badger?"
"All," answered Frigg. "Even the badger."

"Every element? The melting snow as well?"
"All," answered Frigg. "Not a drop of water will hurt him."

"Every plant? All poisons? All nettles?"
"He will not be poisoned," said she. "Nor stung by a nettle."

"All?"
"All, all," Frigg answered, anger revealing itself. "Almost all. Small difference that it makes."

"Ahh," said the crone. "Small? The difference between all and almost all is indeed small. Between victory and close second, small difference. Don't you agree?"

The glare Frigg cast on this crone's visage
Would have melted a glacier.

"One bush of mistletoe," said Frigg.
"West of Valhalla, on the side of a mountain
in the shade of a teetering boulder.
That single sprig of mistletoe is the only spot
in all the nine worlds that promised not."

"Not?" cackled the crone. "That spot?"

"Not for naught that spot," laughed Frigg.
For when the spring thaw comes, and the mountain
ice melts, the boulder will fall and crush the mistletoe.
Then all will have sworn, and Baldur will be safe."

The crone swiftly departed.
And Loki did travel
West of Valhalla to that mountain.

In the shade of the teetering boulder
was found the mistletoe. Mistletoe!

Loki cut the straightest branch from the thin
bush, sharpened its tip
and fashioned a dart.

Back to Asgard Loki went,
humming a careless tune.

Still laughing were the gods.
Hucking and throwing, poking and spearing,
hacking and slashing,
while in their midst, fearless,
Baldur giggled like an innocent young child.

By the side, lonely and sad, stood poor blind Hod,
Baldur's brother.

To Hod, Loki went invisible in disguise,
(not that such was needed to fool the sightless
sibling).

"Why look you so glum Hod, while all the other
gods game and play at target practice with thy
kin?"

"I am blind," said Hod. "I have no weapon.
I cannot play."

"T'would be a shame to miss this game," said the
stranger to Hod.
"Here. Take this dart and try it at Baldur."

"I would miss," said poor glum Hod.
"We will guide thy hand," said the hidden voice.
"Thy aim will be sure and true."

Into the midst of this raucous chaos
Loki led Hod to his brother Baldur's side.
The thin dart Loki placed into Hod's fingers.
Back went Hod's hand, nestled by his ear.
A sightless smile on the blind boy's face.
At last he could play with his brother.

Out flew the dart,
straight and true and through.
Pierced Baldur's spine.

Through Baldur's brain went thought no more.
Through Baldur's heart flowed blood no more.
Baldur the beautiful
stood still for a moment,
gaped at his brother,
then fell forward on his face into the mud.

"Did I hit?" asked blind Hod, cheerfully,
standing, proudly speaking into the silent ring
of dumbfounded gods as his brother's still warm,
body leaked life away

Invisible and watching,
Loki enjoyed his carefully crafted play.

Revels and Reveals

Far from Asgard I stayed
for a year and a day and then word came.
Have you heard the news, sir?
The gods, sir. A feast, sir.
Did they invite you, Loki sir?
No, sir.
Never, sir.
Loki the faithful, Loki the crafty,
Loki the often, nay always, snubbed.

So I crashed the party.
Through the gates I barreled,
Killing a servant who moved too slow.
The gods stared at me in mock dismay.
Those who I once held dear friends.
There Bragi, there Odin, Freya, Frigg,
Heimdall, Thor's wife Sif.

"Cousins. Brothers," I shout. "Good fellows and ladies. Thus arrives Loki late to the feast, raise your mugs high, and drink a toast to his health."

"You are not welcome," says Odin, the allfather.

"Brother-in-blood, say I. "The maker of mirth not hugged to thy side? Why?"

"Make peace," Odin says, "and we will stay our anger."

"Peace? You ask me for Peace, my blood brother? Who was it betrayed my family on the words of witches?"

"Prevention," says old One-Eye, never denying the charge. "Cut off a limb to thwart gangrene. Tis better to die in battle than in sickened sleep."

"Aye," says Bragi, "But cowardly Loki would know little of battle."

"Bragi the braggart," says Loki. "Bragi is a cowering god. First to raise his voice, last to raise his sword. Trembles behind his shield and shouts, 'On! On!' while watching the backsides of heroes.

"I'd slay you right now," says Bragi.

But Freya, Fair Freya, of course, stays Bragi's trembling hand. "Peace, Loki," says the fair goddess. "We offer hospitality, begrudge it not."

"Hospitality from the whore of the gods!
Freya, who would pledge her hospitality for a bit of jewelry – though not for a castle wall?
Freya is truly hospitable, and quite good in bed.
Mmmm. Almost as tasty as good grieving Frigg,
moaning softly, who betrayed her son for a bit of quiet."

"Silence!" bellow's white bearded Heimdall.
"Insult not your betters!"

"Betters? Any snail is better than a god so dull he steadfastly stands watch, forever waiting for the end of the world.

"Any dung beetle is better than those who
pick prophecy over friendship,
revel in slaughter and destruction,
and spurn Loki's laughter and wit,
though they willingly and frequently profit by it."

"At least," whispers Sif, slender wife of Thor
"He finds me blameless of all."

"Blameless? You, Sif? The Thunder God's doxy?
The Hammerhead's ball and chain?
Well, Sif, I have tasted your wares,

and I did find them blameless, though bland.
I wonder what the Dundergod would do
if knew he I know all the secrets you hold…
That tattooed lightning bolt on your inner left thigh?"

"Cease!" roars Thor, thudhead.
"Thy prattle does near to offend."

"Only near, Thor? Is not my aim true, Thor?
Count thy sons, Thor. Number they all thine?
You bluster and blow. Your thunder shakes the
earth, but I've seen thee cower in a glove, bested
by an old woman and unable to lift a pussycat.

"Thou knowst the truth, Loki," says Thor.

"Aye, Thor," say I. "I've tasted the wares both of thy
wife and thou. Can't say which I preferred more."

"Lies!" Thor shouts.

"A shape shifterer am I. Think on it.
All thy bedside secrets.
How else would I know that thou Thor bears the
twin of Sif's lightning bolt tattooed on your inner
right thigh?

"Loki has feasted on the gods. Every one.
A bountiful table. Pillows and fluff.
Yet I know a giantess, Angrboda, now dead,
who I count more manly than Thor."

"Speak plainly," says Thor,
never one to catch hidden meaning.

"I fucked your wife," say I.
"And in disguise, I have fucked you, too.
Your love hammer, thy mighty Mjölnir, is quite small.

Momentarily wordless was Thor.
Paralyzed with rage.

Slay their kin and they are angered.
Seduce their women and offend their prowess,
or offend their women and seduced their prowess
and they go mad.

In any case, the chase was on.
All of Asgard gave pursuit.
Loki fled. The gods followed.

Over land, under sea, cross the sky…
Through Midgard and back.

I could tell you how I eluded the gods, escaped,
dodged, tricked, backtrailed, ambushed…
A wonderful adventure, full of near-death thrills.

Yet even Loki grows tired of his own cleverness.
They caught me in a fish story.

I was tired. Tired of running.
I changed myself into a salmon to cool off and
rest. I was sunning myself in a pool of icy water.

They say fish do not sleep, yet I dozed.

My nap gave Odin his chance,
and in a net of my own folly,
Loki was captured.

Smoked out as a salmon was Loki the fox,
and became, dare I say it, Loki lox.

Bound

My punishment was as Vala had seen. And more.

They slew my oldest boy, Sigyn's son, Nari,
(who I really didn't know very well)
and tied me to a boulder with Nari's entrails.

My back was bent, arms and legs pulled tight.
I could not shape shift away.

Above my face they hung a serpent,
acid venom slowly dripping from its fangs.

Now, I watch as each dribble forms a heavy drop.
And then falls.

Stupid faithful Sigyn, my mourning wife,
reaches a wooden bowl up to catch the plopping
poison before it splashes.

Eventually, the bowl fills, and Sigyn must empty it.
No matter how quickly she hurries,
never fast enough.
Shit that hurts! The earth quakes with my agony
as the poison scars my cheeks.

For a time, the gods stand watch in silent circle,
satisfied that, at last,
the prophecy was fulfilled.

"Now Loki," Thor whispers in my ear,
"this is thy bed. Enjoy thy rest."

One by one they leave me,
bound until time's finish,
alone to my screams,
and my doltish bride's babbles.

Odin last, looks one-eyed, then turns away,
and is gone.

So, Prometheus, what are you in for?
Bringing fire to the world of men?
Such folly.

I? Oh, Aye.
Clever Loki dared a feat far more foolish.
Bringing grins to the gods.
Guffaws to the giants.
Joy to the world of men.
Wit and wisdom entwined.
The joke's on me.
I scream with laughter but cannot flee.

Ragnarok

What? Listen.
Is that Heimdall's horn I hear?
Faint hope rising like gorge…
It is!
It was said these bonds would hold until the end
of the world.
Will they break? Almost. Soon.

But Heimdall's trumpet must sound three times.
Listen. Was that twice?
It was!
Soon. Another.
One more. Come on. Come now, blow…

The sleepless watchman finally sees his doom
approach, and again, again?
It will be!
The blast echoes!
Three. Thrice! Done.
At last!
Ragnarok!

Loki's shackles shatter.
They break, I stand.

Scarred but unbroken.
A quick kiss for my screaming wife
(deeply, with acid-scarred tongue).
It's time people! Giants, gods!
To battle!

The lull is past.
The age of gods and giants is ending.
Into the fields of death we stride.
Gods from the West ride against
giants from the East.

And though I'd still rather war with wit than weapons,
Loki, with his daughter, Hel rides proudly on the prow of a ship made from the nail parings of the dead! Our family has style!

Campfires extinguished, bodies strewn,
now the fields wash red with blood and gore.

My son, wolf Fenris has eaten the sun!
My son, world-serpent Jormungand has let loose his tail and prowls for prey.

The armies of the giants assemble and charge
And the motley lot of gods do tremble and fall.

Time for the gods to die.
All according to the prophecy.
How's all that foreknowledge doing for ya now,
Odin?

Look! Fenris loosed from his bonds leaps forward,
fangs bared.
Sic 'em boy. Go for the throat.
There falls Odin – the half-blind all-father –
his ancient bearded neck torn asunder.
My son Fenris the wolf eats the heart of his
godfather, his betrayer, who broke his mother's heart.
The Eldest god's blood dripping from his snout,
Fenris howls in fury as Odin's twin ravens pluck at
his eyes.

There!
Thor, his hammer, the mighty Mjölnir, raised.
Now! Jormungand, my long long long lost son,
has closed his teeth, his ginormous jaws,
around Thor's boots, britches, balls, hands and
head, and swallows.
Lightning strikes no more.
Thunder echoes no more.
Yet, wait… No!
Thor hammers a hole through my son's serpentine
stomach.

Thor takes nine stumbling steps and then dies at last, entwined in poor Jormungand's intestines.

One by one they all fall.
Dismembered Freya, lovely no more.
Tyr is dead. Bragi is dead. Sif is dead.
Blind Hod falls off a cliff.

And resting on a hill in the midst of the fray,
Loki the trickster, both god and giant,
drinks in the delicious carnage of his creation.

Then Heimdall the dullard steps before Loki,
And while I skewer Heimdall, he skewers me.

I watch as we both die.
It feels like a painful metaphor. Boredom and freedom intertwined at the end of time.
Feh.
Ow.

I watch.
Now the flood.
Fire and ice sweep across the world and the battlefield draws silent, save for the crows feasting on freshly iced eyeballs.

They say that from all this carnage
will arise a new world.
Another fucking prophecy.

They say that Odin's long lost sons, Villi and Ve
will rescue Baldur and Hod from the underworld,
and that two hidden humans,
Lif and Lifthrasir will repeople the Earth.

Ahh.
An idyllic garden filled with dull joy.
It could be nice I think.
Fair and green and quiet,
quiet and green,
purged of pain and hate. Safe.
No wickedness nor laughter.
O beautiful beginning.

Will such a peace ever be?
We shall see. We shall see.

About the Author

Mark Binder is a graduate of Columbia University, where he studied mythology with David Damrosch and T. E. Gaster and storytelling with Spalding Gray. He received an MA in Theater and English from Rhode Island College, and is a graduate of the Trinity Rep Theater Conservatory.

Over the years, he has edited newspapers and magazines, started small theaters, repaired windows, taught at schools and universities, and toured as a performance storyteller, spinning tales for listeners of all ages around the world.

He has written and recorded more than 20 books and audio books for adults, families and children.

Mark lives in Providence with his wife and family.

For more about Mark Binder books and audio recordings,
speaking tours and story concerts,
and for unique and rare stories
please visit
http://markbinder.com

Loki Ragnarok

Thanks to Adam Gertsacov for inspiration and friendship. Thanks to Marvel Comics and the Ancient Norse for the myths. Thanks to Elspeth Kovar, Bob Whelan and Laura Packer for their feedback. Thanks to George Dussault for listening.

Softcover ISBN: 978-1-940060-27-9
eBook ISBN: 978-1-940060-26-2
Printed in the USA • 10 9 8 7 6 5 4 3 2 1

Light Publications
PO Box 2462
Providence, RI 02906
U. S. A.
http://lightpublications.com

www.ingramcontent.com/pod-product-compliance
Lightning Source LLC
Chambersburg PA
CBHW030544310726
48979CB00010B/2019/J

9781940060286